GW01018535

JACK THE ST.
AND
THE LOST KITTENS

ALAN CLIFF

Half author royalties to
Save the Family

printed & published by
Gwasg Helygain Ltd
68-70 Kinmel Street, Rhyl, Denbighshire LL18 1AW
01745 331411

Author: Alan Cliff, 2005-2008 ©
Front Cover and Internal Art: Nigel Cliff, 2005-2008 ©
Guest Illustrator: Jessica Jones, County Conwy, 2005-2008 ©
Puzzles: Brenda Wyatt, 2005-2008 ©

1st printed 2005
2nd edition 2008

ISBN 978 09550338 0 3

Printed & Published by:
Gwasg Helygain Ltd., 68-70 Kinmel Street,
Rhyl, Denbighshire LL18 1AW
Tel: 01745 331411 Fax: 01745 331310
Trade enquiries & book orders welcome.
E-mail: info@gwasg.com
Website: www.gwasg.com

British Library Cataloguing-in-Publication Data
A catalogue record for this book is available from the British Library.

Trademark Notice: 'Jack the Station Cat' is registered
for trademark purposes.

www.jackthestationcat.co.uk
Order books online at: www.gwasg.com

Railway 'Jack Days' may be organised.
Please visit the Jack website in the first instance.

Reading guide: 5-8 year olds

Registered Charity No. 516484
Company Registration No. 1908006

gemma.ryder@savethefamily.uk.com
www.savethefamily.uk.com

About Save the Family

Save the Family is a local charity providing sheltered accommodation for homeless families in North Wales, Cheshire, The Wirral and Merseyside. The families supported by this unique charity have fallen off the bottom of the social ladder. Without Save the Family, the only alternative would be for their children to be taken into care.

These families come from the poorest 10% of neighborhoods in the UK; estates with endemic unemployment, domestic violence, drug or alcohol abuse, poor health, unsuitable housing conditions, high levels of debt and low educational attainment. At our existing centre at Plas Bellin Hall in Flintshire, Save the Family works to restore self-respect and teach basic life skills, while addressing the root causes of repeat homelessness. The goal is to give parents back their hope and give their children a future.

Every night, 150 people depend on Save the Family for a roof over their heads. More than half of these are children. We have supported more than 5,000 families since 1976, but we only have space to accommodate 12% of those referred to us. That's why we're building a new centre for 26 families at Cotton Hall Farm, near Chester – because we want to do more. Every donation we receive goes towards making a difference to a local family, enabling people to rebuild shattered lives and avoid becoming homeless again.

For more information, visit Save the Family's web site at www.savethefamily.uk.com or call 01244 333490. Those interested in our work are welcome to visit our facilities by prior arrangement.

Trust Chairwoman: Mrs Edna Speed MBE
Save the Family Ltd, Abbey House, Abbey Green, Chester CH1 2JH
Tel: 01244 409100   Fax: 01244 409200

June 2008

Dear Boys & Girls...

Welcome to "Jack The Station Cat and the Lost Kittens" an old favourite. I hope you like the new coloured illustrations.

In this book you will find five cats; Jack, Aunty Buzz, Cousin Tom and the twin kittens Marmalade and Myfanwy. Over twenty-five years cats with these names have lived with us.

If you go to Porthmadog on North Wales you will find the little narrow gauge line called the Welsh Highland Railway. Look out for locomotives Gelert and Russell. You might just see Cousin Tom helping drive one of them.

Did you know lots of stations really had station cats? Some still do. If you find one, do write and tell me.

Enjoy Jack and his family's adventure and then try the puzzles at the end of the book.

Alan Cliff

JACK THE STATION CAT
AND
THE LOST KITTENS

"Scritch, scratch, scrunge." Jack the Station Cat sharpened his claws on an old wooden sleeper in the yard at Tail's End station. He stretched this way and that. "That's better," he sighed.

"Woof, woof!" A large silver grey dog appeared. Jack jumped on to a stack of crates. "Newcomer," he thought. He watched the dog pick his way over the bumpy yard.

"Good morning. I'm Jack the Station Cat," he miaowed.

"I'm Jack the Station Cat"

"Hello, I'm Wyn. My **proper** name is Whitford Wyn the Fifth. I'm a weimaraner," said the dog rather haughtily.

"No need to show off," said Jack. "**My** proper name is Jackson Purrkins and an ancestor of mine tamed a dragon."

"**My** ancestors were used for hunting in Germany: wild cats a speciality."

"Spitttz," snarled Jack and arched his back. "You hunt **cats**?" he growled.

"Don't worry," said the dog. "I'm not going to hunt you. Quite used to cats, you know."

Just then a lady appeared by the big gates at the yard entrance. "Wyn," she called.

"Dilys, my human," said the dog. "See you again." He loped away.

Jack went to find his Aunty Buzz. The old cat was sitting on a porter's trolley. "Hello, Dear Boy," she purred. "You seem to be in a hurry."

"Aunty! Aunty! I have just met a big dog who hunts cats and he's called Wyn."

"Did he say what sort of dog?" Aunty

enquired.

"A weimaraner," replied Jack.

"Station master at Much Purring had one years ago," said Aunty Buzz. "So long as he thought he was Top Animal he didn't bother anyone. By the way, your Cousin Tom is coming to stay for a few days and those twin kittens Marmalade and Myfanwy should be with him."

"Oh no!" groaned Jack. "The kittens are really naughty and Cousin Tom thinks he's a sailor. I suppose they're on the train that's just arriving."

Jack and Aunty trotted along the platform to the guard's van. "There's Tom," shouted Jack.

"Shiver my timbers, if it isn't Jack and Aunty Buzz," roared an enormous cat. He was black with a white chin and front and four huge white paws. "There's a sou'wester blowing up, my hearties. Reef the tops'ls."

"Thomas, stop talking nonsense," said Aunty Buzz severely. "It's nice to see you but where are Marmalade and Myfanwy?"

Tom looked round. "Avast, ye landlubbers," he roared. Nothing happened, not a kitten to be seen.

"Perhaps they're asleep"

"Perhaps they're asleep," suggested Jack. The three cats looked through the door of the guard's van. "Marmy, Mivvy," they called. There was nobody there.

"Man the lifeboats. Kittens overboard," yelled Tom.

"Thomas, stop this sailor talk. The only ships you've been on are a barge on the Llangollen canal and a yacht at Porthmadog," said Aunty staring at him.

"Sorry, Aunty." The big cat hung his head. "I think I've lost the kittens. They were definitely with me when we left Mews Junction. Marmalade was pulling my tail."

"I think they must have sneaked off at Much Purring. It's the only station between here and The Junction," said Jack. "I expect you were asleep, Tom." Tom looked guilty. "Let's contact Much Purring. We'll ask Gareth the snail to send a message via ESP (Electronic Snail Post)" continued Jack. Tom and Jack scampered along the platform while Aunty Buzz trundled behind.

...on his favourite stone ...

They found Gareth on his favourite stone in the Tail's End station garden. A little notice at the end of the stone read:

Sir Gareth, Cornish Railway Snail.

Messages sent and received.

Problems quickly solved.

"Morning Gareth," said Jack. "My Cousin Tom needs your help."

"What's your problem, Tom?" asked the snail.

"I've lost two kittens, Marmalade and Myfanwy. They gave me the slip when the train stopped at Much Purring."

"Very careless of you, Tom. Still, don't worry. I will ask my brother Sir Gawain at Much Purring to make enquiries."

The cats sat in a circle round the stone. Gareth disappeared into his shell.

Fizz! Fizz! Sparks flew and a blue light shone round the snail's shell.

"The ESP is working," whispered Jack to Tom.

The big cat was about to say "Well, I'll be keelhauled," when he saw Aunty Buzz had a severe look in her eye. He purred instead.

Eventually after much fizzing there was a loud pop. Gareth's head appeared. "No sign of them," he announced.

... glumly returned to the platform ...

The cats glumly returned to the platform. "Jack!" bellowed Cousin Tom, "there's a big silver grey dog coming."

"That's Wyn the weimaraner," breathed Jack.

"Well, well," muttered Aunty. "Kindly introduce the hound to me, Jack. Tom stay here. If we need help we'll yell."

Scritch. Scratch. Scrunge. "I'm sharpening my cutlasses. I mean my claws, Aunty," growled

Tom.

"Hello Wyn," said Jack. "Meet my Aunty Buzz."

"Aunty Buzz? Aunty Buzz!" replied the dog. "My grandfather Whitford Wyn the Third said if ever I met a black and white cat called Aunty Buzz I was to give her any help I could. At your service, Madam."

"Grandpa and I were great friends," smiled Aunty. "Now Wyn, we've lost two kittens at Much Purring."

"I'll help you find them," announced the dog.

"What about your human?" objected Jack.

"Leave Dilys to me. She's quite clever for a human." The big dog stood on his hind legs and put a paw on Dilys's shoulder. He pointed the other paw at the cats. "Wuff! Wuff!" he barked. He then pointed at the train. "Wuff! Wuff!"

"You want to go on the train with the cats?" asked Dilys.

Wyn woofed. He winked at the cats. Dilys

called to George the Guard. "Wyn wants to go on the train with the cats."

"Good idea, Dilys," replied George. "We've lost two kittens at Much Purring. Wyn and the cats will soon find them." George opened the guard's door. "In you go," he shouted. Wyn gave a huge leap and vanished into a pile of mail bags. "Mmmmf, mmmmf! Get me out of here," he mumbled. Aunty Buzz waddled through the door. "Foolish dog! Just like your grandfather. Sit up and behave," she said. Wyn heaved himself out of the mail bags. "Sorry, Aunty."

"Sorry, Aunty"

"Come along Boys and stop sniggering," called Aunty. Jack and Tom obeyed.

"All aboard!" shouted George. "Wrexham train. First stop Much Purring."

Peep! Peep! George blew his whistle and waved his green flag. Away went the train.

"Out you get," said George to Wyn and the cats when the train reached Much Purring. "See if you can find the lost kittens before the train gets back."

"This is where your grandfather was Station Dog years ago, Wyn," called Aunty.

Wyn pricked up his ears. "Aaaraagh, aaarowww. **This is a job for Super Dog!**" he howled. Aunty Buzz was very, very cross. "Wyn, you are a naughty dog just like your grandfather," growled Aunty. Wyn looked sheepish. He wagged his little tail. "Sorry, Aunty. But I really can help. Let's go to the other platform where the kittens probably jumped out. I'll soon sniff where they have gone."

When they had clambered over the bridge Aunty was tired. She curled up on a seat in the sun. "Find the kittens, Boys," she said. Zzzz! Zzzz! Aunty was asleep.

Wyn ran up and down the platform. Sniff! Sniff! Snuffle! Snuffle! Suddenly he stopped. "This way," he barked, and raced out of the station into a field. Jack and Tom scampered after the dog. Sniff! Sniff! Snuffle! Snuffle! The weimaraner with his nose to the ground crossed the field. "The kittens went into this wood," he called.

"Good work, Wyn," shouted Jack.

The dog and the two cats plunged into the wood. Crackle! Crackle! Dried leaves broke up under their paws. It was gloomy as not much sun came through the trees. Wyn kept going. Crash! Crackle! The dog pushed his way further into the wood. Jack and Tom followed, their eyes gleaming green, their fur standing up and their tails switching.

"Halt!" said a voice. "Going somewhere?" It was Fawcett the Fox.

"If you must know, Fox, we are a Search and Rescue party," said Jack. "We are looking for two lost kittens. Have you seen them?"

"Do you mean a stripey ginger kitten and a tortoiseshell one?"

"That's right," replied Jack.

"He's locked them up," squeaked a voice from above. It was Rusty the Red Squirrel.

"He's locked them up"

"Oh no I haven't!" yelled the fox.

"Ooooh yesss yooouu have," hooted Ozimandius the Owl as he floated past looking like a white ghost.

"Oh no I haven't!" squealed the fox.

Clump! Clump! Clump! "Oh yes you did," grunted a deep voice. "What's more, I've let them out and here they are, riding on my back."

" ... here they are, riding on my back"

"Hello, Uncle Jack. Hello, Uncle Tom." The two kittens slid off the badger's back. "The fox shut us up in his gaol. He said we were trespassers and he was a policeman," announced Marmalade. "This kind badger let us out when he heard us crying."

"Broughton the badger is a Very Important Animal," added Myfanwy.

Fawcett the Fox looked very uncomfortable.

Scritch. Scratch. Scrunge. Jack sharpened his claws on some wood.

"I didn't mean them any harm," coughed Fawcett nervously. "I just kept them safe. Looking after lost kittens is a policeman's duty."

"Fawcett is a bit heavy pawed," said the badger. "He means well but he should have brought Marmalade and Myfanwy to me first."

Marmalade and Myfanwy

Jack and Tom were so happy to find the kittens. They thanked the woodland animals.

"On my back, kittens," said Wyn lying down. "We'll take you back to the station."

"We're doing well for rides today, Twin," squeaked Marmalade. "A train, a badger, and now a great big dog." When they got to the station they found Aunty Buzz waiting for them.

"Why did you get off the train, kittens?" asked Jack.

"Uncle Tom is always telling us about Porthmadog. He says it's a wonderful place with ships, two narrow gauge railways and a big railway," said Marmalade.

"Uncle Tom says he used to sail out of Porthmadog to far away places," added Myfanwy. "That's when he wasn't driving **Gelert** and **Russell**, two engines on the little railway by the big station . . .

. . . driving Gelert . . .

" . . . It's called the Welsh Highland Railway
. . ." interrupted Marmalade.

" . . . We thought the station we stopped at
might be Porthmadog. Uncle Tom was asleep so we
got off and went 'sploring. It was exciting."
Marmalade nodded his head. "We didn't find a
little railway or any ships, but we did find a wood
and we were locked up," finished Myfanwy.

"Thomas!" boomed Aunty Buzz, "what have you been telling these kittens?"

"Don't be cross with Uncle Tom," said Marmalade and Myfanwy together. "He tells lovely stories, and we really shouldn't have got off the train."

Whoo! Whoo! An engine whistle sounded. "That's the Tail's End train coming," cried Jack.

The train pulled into the platform. "Come along, cats, come along Wyn," shouted George the Guard. "I see you've found the kittens."

Soon they were back at Tail's End. "Now Twins, say thank you," said Jack.

"Thank you, Wyn," said the kittens. "You **were** clever to find us." Lick, lick. Lick, lick. They washed the big dog's face. "What sort of dog are you?" whispered Marmalade. "Uncle Jack seemed to say you were a 'wild man's army', but there's only one of you."

The weimaraner laughed. "I can be very wild if you want. Aaarrgghhooo! Arrrghooo! **That was a job for Super Dog**," he howled as he rushed down the platform.

"Just like his grandfather," murmured Aunty Buzz.

Super Dog

The End

This picture of Whitford Wyn the Fifth the weimaraner is by student Jessica Jones of County Conwy.

Now draw **your** picture of Wyn below.

PUZZLES

1) **DOGS**

A Weimaraner is a dog used when hunting. It has a very short grey coat and a short tail.

It is named after a city in Germany called **'WEIMAR'**.

Can you sort out the following 3 names of other German breeds of dog?

a) **HASCUDDNH** _ _ _ _ _ _ _ _ _

b) **OTWIERERTL** _ _ _ _ _ _ _ _ _ _

c) **ILSTAAAN** _ _ _ _ _ _ _ _

Clues - **not** in order!

One is also known as a **German Shepherd Dog**

One is a large strongly built dog often used as a guard

One is sometimes known as a **Sausage Dog**

Hint: On a piece of scrap paper put the letters round **in a circle**

d) In which of these continents is Germany?

Asia / Africa / Europe / North and South America / Antarctica / Australia

_____

2) **OPPOSITES**

In the story you will find several opposites. Write them below.

IN

NAUGHTY

LITTLE

LOST

ON

STOOD

FRONT

OPEN

NO

_____

3) **COUNTING**
Count the total number of **animals, snails** and **birds**
who are **named** in this story

_____

Take away the number of **words on the notice**
at the end of Gareth's stone

_____

Add the number of "**humans**" whose **names** we are told

_____

Where in the story is the answer number you have found?
(clue: look at the guard's van)

_____

4) **TWOS**

a)   Name the two **kittens**

b)   Name the two **engines**

c)   Name the two **uncles**

d)   Name the two **snails**

e)   One of the above four 'twos' is different.
Spot the odd "pair"

_____

5)   **Whitford Wyn the fifth used**

this to point with . . .   _____

this to wink with . . .   _____

this to sniff with . . .   _____

The first letters of your answer will spell what you've
probably used to complete these puzzles!!!

ANSWERS

1) a) Dachshund   b) Rottweiler   c) Alsatian   d) Europe

2) In/OUT   Naughty/GOOD   Little/BIG   Lost/FOUND   On/OFF
Stood/SAT   Front/BACK   Open/SHUT   No/YES

3) Animals: 1) Whitford Wyn the 5th 2) Jack 3) Aunty Buzz 4) Tom 5)
Marmalade 6) Myfanwy 7)Whitford Wyn the 3rd 8) Fawcett 9) Rusty 10)
Broughton **Snails:** 11) Gareth 12) Gawain **Bird:** 13) Ozimandius = 13.
Less: Number of words on poster = 12.
Plus: Number of named humans **Dilys** and **George** = 2.
13-12 = 1, 1+1 = 2 = 3
"The **three** cats looked through the door."

4) a)   Marmalade and Myfanwy
b)   **Gelert and Russell**
c)   Jack and Tom
d)   Gareth and Gawain
e)   Odd ones out (they are not alive) **Gelert and Russell**

5) **Paw, Eye, Nose . . . Pen**